A FRIEND FOR MINERVA LOUISE

Janet Morgan Stoeke

DUTTON CHILDREN'S BOOKS • NEW YORK

Copyright © 1997 by Janet Morgan Stoeke
All rights reserved.
CIP Data is available.

Published in the United States 1997
by Dutton Children's Books,
a division of Penguin Books USA Inc.
375 Hudson Street, New York, New York 10014

Designed by Ellen M. Lucaire
Printed in Hong Kong • First Edition
2 4 6 8 10 9 7 5 3 1
ISBN 0-525-45869-7

For Elliott Morgan Brooks

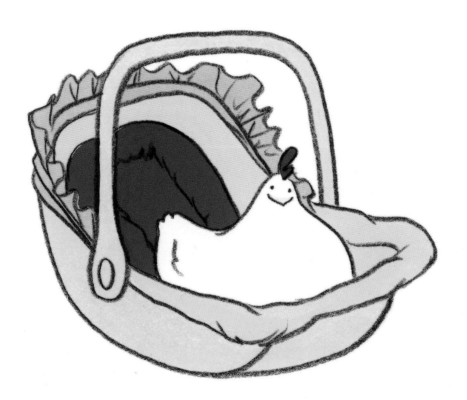

The house with the red curtains looks
different today, thought Minerva Louise.

What is it?

Oh, they have a new wheelbarrow. Isn't it fancy!

I wonder what else has changed around here.

That fence wasn't there before.

And look—a new rabbit hutch.

There must be a new bunny here.
I wonder where he is.

Have you seen the new bunny?

He's not under the gardening workbench.

And he's not in this cozy little nest.

He must be around here somewhere.

Hmm. If I were a bunny, I might
squeeze under the fence . . .

and look around for a way to get outdoors.

That's it. He went out past those flowers.

Hey, he has another pen in the yard!

Wait a minute. This is a fishpond.

I wish I could find that bunny.
We could have so much fun together.

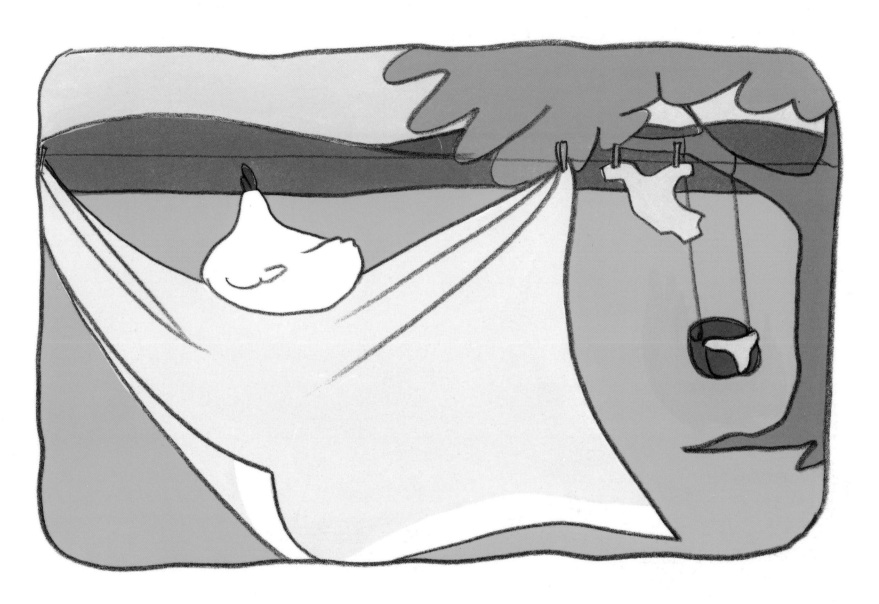

He would love this swing.
You can see the whole world from up here.

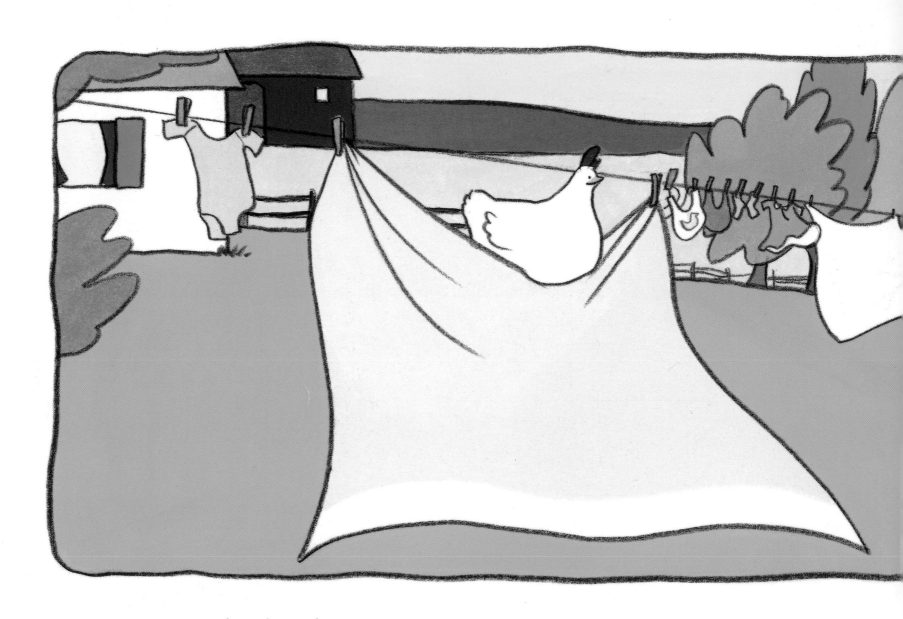

Oh, look. Here come the farmers.
They've got something in the wheelbarrow.

I hope it's the bunny!

It *is!* And he's got some great toys with him!